Danny and the Runaway Train

written and photographed
by
Mia Coulton

Danny and Bee
like to play
with the big train.

3

Look at Bee
on the train.

Bee is going
around and around
on the train.

The train is going
faster and faster.

Bee is going
faster and faster
on the train.

Here comes Bee again.

Bee is going
around and around.

The train is going
faster and faster.

Oh, no!

Look at the track!

The train will go off
the track, and Bee is
on the train!

Oh, no!

The train is off

the track!

It is a *runaway train*!

"I got you, Bee,"
said Danny.
"I got you off
the *runaway train*."

"I got you off

just in time!"